Out of Water

Out of Water

FROM THE COLLECTION
SHAPES IN THE DARK
18 QUEER HORROR STORIES
BY WILLIAM JACKSON

Cambridge
Queer Press

First published in 2024 by the Cambridge Queer Press
an imprint of MFco Ltd. Unit 4 City Limits, Danehill, Reading
RG6 4UP, UK.

ISBN 978-1-912622-51-1

Text is set in Cormorant Garamond 13pt on 19pt.

Out of Water

"Nature is so linked together,

that the ocean imitates the land,

And leaves us in astonishment to stand."

What have we here? A man or a fish.
Flyer, Phoenix Printing Office, Lambeth, 1887

PROTEE

A warm breeze scattered clouds of sand across the shore. Pearl-tipped combers ran hard against the beach, drawing up the wave-wet shingle as they retreated. Matt walked absent-mindedly, swallowed up by the vast emptiness of the beach and its wildness.

He noticed something lying at the wave line, tangled and stranded, unmoving in the day's dying light. He thought it might be a resting seal - or a dead one. As he got closer, he saw its human nakedness. And he began to run.

He bent over the still figure. A boy, probably in his late teens. Matt cradled him gently. The boy's hair was silver-blond, like steel, his skin pale as pearl, catching the soft hues of early evening. His jaw was strong and dimpled. His face was impossibly young, heroic even. Matt stroked the boy's cheek to rouse him and he opened his large dark eyes.

'Are you all right? What happened? Were you out swimming?'

The boy just looked at him and blinked. He was trembling.

'Let's get you into the warm.'

*

By the time they got to the beach house, the shoreline had greyed behind them and the embers of the day were glowing faintly at the horizon. Matt laid the boy on the bed and

What have we here? A man or a fish.

Vide Shakspeare's "Tempest."

Just arrived in this kingdom, and lately exhibited at the Surrey Zoological Gardens, to thousands of admiring Spectaters,

---

A REAL

MERMAID

AND

MERMAN!

CAUGHT ALIVE

In a Bay, after a Storm, by a Tribe of Indians, near the spot were the "Wager" (Man of War) was wrecked some years ago, the most desolate part of the World, termed TERRA DEL FUEGO, the Southernmost part of South America. They were purchased from the Indians by Captain Brown, of the "Good Intent," South Sea Whaler, and landed in London.

The wonderful production of a Foreign Clime, combining the HUMAN FORM and FISH together, They are near 4ft. in length, the upper part completely human to the waist; the Female of a pleasing brunette countenance. The Male bears a striking likeness to the Indians, the arms and hair are long, they are webbed between the fingers, in place of ears Nature has supplied them with gills; the lower or fish part is covered with large strong scales; two large fins under the breasts support them in an upright position in the water—the Dorsal and Tail Fins are very powerful.—The Seal is said to be half a Dog and Fish, the Monkey imitates Man, and the Bat is Bird and Beast,

> "Nature is so linked together, that the ocean imitates the land,
> And leaves us in astonishment to stand."

Nature is wonderful in all her works.

Creatures of this species have been often seen on the Coast of Norway, Scotland, and Ireland, by hundreds of living witnesses.

The Proprietor will take the liberty of calling for this Bill in the course of the day, to give you an opportunity of seeing them.

Your recommendation to a friend will confer a favor. Schools and Families attended at any fixed time. Please to give this Bill to the family. N.B.—The ancient Poets describe them as Syrens sitting and singing on the Rocks of Scylla and Charybidis, to seduce unwary mariners to destruction.

Phœnix Printing Office, 4, Upper Marsh, Lambeth.

covered him with a blanket. He made hot tea and the boy drank it eagerly.

'Careful,' Matt said, 'or you'll burn your mouth. What's your name?'

The boy smiled, 'I don't know.'

'You don't know your own name? Have you been in an accident? What were you doing out there on the beach?'

'I was in the water. I love the water.'

'Where are your clothes?'

'I don't have any.'

'You don't have any clothes? I think you may have taken a knock on the head, sunshine. Maybe we should get you looked at.'

'No,' the boy grasped Matt's wrist. 'No. Please, don't. I'm okay.'

'All right, but let me get you something to eat.'

Matt gave the boy a tee shirt, socks and sweatpants. The sweatpants were slightly too

big and Matt pulled the drawstring tight to keep them from sliding down the boy's narrow hips. They went into the kitchen.

'What's the last thing you remember before I found you?' Matt heated passata and put some rigatoni on to boil.

'Swimming to the shore,' the boy said. 'I wanted to see the shore.'

'Nothing before that?'

'No.'

'And you don't know your name?'

The boy shook his head. There was something oddly unworldly about him.

'Well, I think I'm going to call you Dylan. It's a Welsh name. Means *son of the sea*.'

'I like it.'

*

The boy wandered around the house, touching furniture and ornaments, even doors and windows as if seeing them for the first time. Matt grated parmesan over the bowls of steaming pasta and took them to the dining table.

'Dig in.' He speared a tube of rigatoni with his fork. Dylan reached into his bowl with his hand.

'No! You'll burn yourself.'

Matt waved his fork in front of Dylan, indicating the fork beside the boy's napkin. Dylan examined it carefully, then stabbed a piece of pasta and put it in his mouth.

He began asking questions. Lots of questions. Did Matt live on the beach? How many other people lived there? What foods did they eat? What did they do with their time?

Did he think all people might live in the sea one day? Some of the questions were so bizarre, Matt thought the boy might really be a bit mad.

'You'd better get some sleep. You can have my bed,' Matt said.

'What about you?'

'I can sleep on the couch.'

'It doesn't look very comfortable.'

'I'll be okay.'

'No, I want you to sleep in the bed too.'

'I shouldn't.'

'Why not?'

Matt couldn't think of a reason. Dylan was beautiful. He wanted to be close to him. 'Well, if you're okay with it?'

'I am.'

They lay down and Matt pulled the covers over them. He felt Dylan take his hand and gently rub his thumb back and forth across his

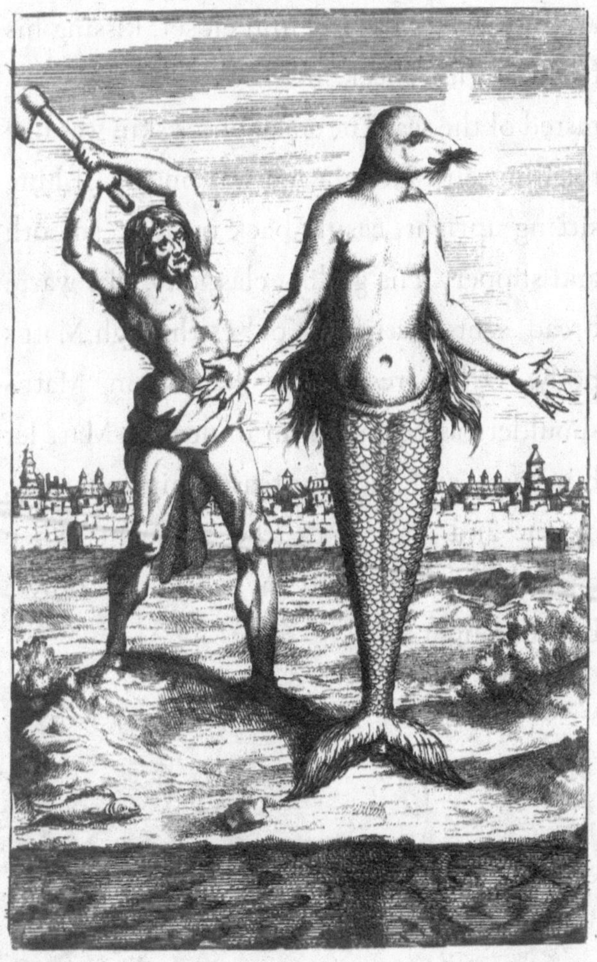

palm. Matt grew hard quickly. He put his arm around Dylan, pulling him closer, kissing his forehead, his cheek, his neck. The boy's lips tasted of the sea. The smell of his skin was like foaming surf. Now Dylan was on top of him, sitting upright, easing back on him, smooth and slippery. His gliding elasticity, like warm bread, sent electrifying pulses through Matt's body. Dylan rested his hands on Matt's shoulders as he took him in deeper. Matt let him lead, and the boy teased him onwards, closer and closer to the moment when everything surged and the world was only a blinding light.

When Matt woke up, he found he was hugging Dylan tight. The morning light had painted the room nectarine bright. He left the boy to sleep. From the porch, he watched the sun cast its first diamonds into the sea.

Dylan wanted to swim after breakfast. They walked hand in hand along the beach. The air was hot, the water warm and vivid under a cerulean sky. Dylan stripped naked and waded into the surf, his shins and ankles spattered by the tide's frothy margins. Matt splashed after him, aroused, churning up the salty water as he swam towards the boy. Dylan turned, waving and beckoning. Matt reached out but the boy disappeared underwater, looping around him like a young seal. Matt dived, and opened his eyes as Dylan kissed him. They twisted downwards, deeper and deeper

into the soundless underworld.

Matt felt the sudden need for air, tensed against the instinct to panic. Dylan pushed his tongue into Matt's mouth, breathing into him, working Matt's hardness with his fingers. Matt felt his passion erupt, spiky white strands suspended in the cooling water.

They swam back to shore and lay together on the sand. The sky was empty. Matt felt the rising breeze, ample and fresh, teasing his skin as he drifted into sleep.

*

Matt sat up, looking up and down the shoreline, scanning the wide, glimmering sea. The sun was high overhead and there was no sign of the boy. He ran into the surf, shouting Dylan's name but the undulating sea gave nothing away. He felt alone and belittled by the sea's absolute indifference.

Then something flickered in the distant blue. Before Matt could make out what it was, it vanished again. A few moments later he saw it once more, much closer this time: Dylan was darting through the water at an incredible speed. The boy stood up in the shallows and strode towards the beach.

Matt hugged him and kissed him. 'I thought you'd drowned.'

'Why?'

'I couldn't see you.'

'I was just out there. Just under the water.'

'I thought I'd lost you.'

Dylan took Matt's hand and they wandered slowly back towards the beach house, kicking their feet in the surf.

The house was cool and dark after the glare of the beach. Matt made chicken sandwiches and grabbed two Peronis from the fridge. He switched on the television and soon felt Dylan's head heavy against his shoulder. He guessed the boy wasn't used to alcohol.

*

Dylan ran outside and knelt on the sand, breathing in bellyfuls of fresh air. He felt sick and dizzy and his head ached.

'I shouldn't have given you beer,' Matt said. 'I'm sorry.'

'Does everybody drink beer?'

'Not everybody.'

Matt folded his arms around Dylan. 'You smell so good I could eat you up.'

'Matt, let's go back for one last swim before it gets dark.'

They raced each other to the sea.

Rain clouds had gathered to the east and the temperature had dipped, the waves were

rolling more forcefully into shore. Dylan was ahead, powering out into the greying expanse. Matt's arms struck the water, legs whipping up foam behind him. He had to keep stopping to make sure he didn't lose sight of the boy. He turned back towards the beach and saw they were a long way from land now. Matt was a little afraid of the sea's wide plain but also intoxicated by its terrible beauty. Dylan came to him.

'Stay close,' Matt said. 'I don't want to lose you.'

'Do you love me?' Dylan asked him, dark eyes blazing.

'Yes.'

'I need something from you.'

'Anything.'

'I need you to give me your soul. Without it, I'll cease to exist. I'll vanish into the sea forever. Will you do it? Will you give me your soul?'

Matt looked towards the beach. The sun had dipped below the horizon. The land was no more than a thin dark strip against the dusky sky. He took hold of the boy, savouring him. His tangle of wet hair, his long lashes, the cool magenta of his lips.

'Yes,' he whispered. 'I'll give you my soul,'

Dylan kissed him, holding him tight, dragging him quickly down beneath the surface. Deeper and deeper, fathoms deep. Matt's senses gave out as the brutal darkness took him.

*

For a long time, the sea was empty. The only sound was the soulful murmuring of the waves. Then the calm was broken as the boy somersaulted high out of the water, now slicing

Fig. IV.
Satyrus Marinus

back through the surface in an acrobatic downward arc. He came up again, body twisting in the moonlight, his face bright but forlorn. He started to swim purposefully towards the shore.

William Jackson

WILLIAM JACKSON IS A BRITISH AUTHOR OF QUEER HORROR FICTION. HIS CHARACTERS INHABIT A HOMONORMATIVE WORLD IN STARK CONTRAST TO THE HETERONORMATIVITY OF SO MUCH HORROR NARRATIVE. HIS WRITING LOOKS AT OPPRESSION, THE INHERENT SEDUCTIVENESS OF EVIL AND THE CORRUPTION, OR MORAL DECAY, OFTEN MASKED BY BEAUTY.

WWW.WILLIAMJACKSON.UK

THE CAMBRIDGE QUEER PRESS PUBLISHES WILLIAM JACKSON'S MAJOR QUEER HORROR WORKS INCLUDING *SATAN'S LAMP, THE SUGAR PIT* AND THE SHORT STORY COLLECTION *SHAPES IN THE DARK*

WWW.CAMBRIDGEQUEERPRESS.CO.UK

Cambridge
Queer Press

PUBLISHER'S CHOICE

A COLLECTION OF SLIM VOLUMES
SELECTED BY OUR PUBLISHER

No. 1

THE MIRACLE OF PONT-L'ABBÉ
A SHORT STORY FROM THE COLLECTION
STORIES FOR BOYS
BY BARRY STEWART HUNTER

No. 2

THE FIRST MANIFESTO OF SURREALISM
THE STORY OF YVAN GOLL'S MANIFESTO OF SURREALISM
PUBLISHED 14 DAYS BEFORE ANDRÉ BRETON'S
WITH AN ESSAY BY MARTIN FIRRELL

No. 3

OUT OF WATER
A QUEER HORROR STORY FROM THE COLLECTION
SHAPES IN THE DARK
BY WILLIAM JACKSON

No. 4

150 YEARS OF GERTRUDE STEIN
OUR PUBLISHER'S CHOICE FROM THE SHORT
WORKS OF GERTRUDE STEIN TO MARK
150 YEARS SINCE HER BIRTH

No. 5

ALL THE BEAUTIFUL BOYS
AN ORIGINAL SHORT STORY FROM
THE MASTER OF QUEER BRITISH
HORROR, WILLIAM JACKSON

No. 6

HOW TO WRITE LIKE MRS WOOLF
C. FARR ON HOW A WRITER
MIGHT SET OUT TO CREATE
RATHER THAN IMITATE FORM

Cambridge
Queer Press